What is Indiana Jones

in December 1916?

Indy's facing tough choices!

While World War I rages in Europe, the same enemies struggle for land in Africa. Land that each side is ordering its native African troops to defend—and die for.

As an officer in the Belgian army, Indy's torn in two directions. How can he carry out heartless orders without betraying the men he commands?

Catch the whole story of Young Indy's travels on the amazing fact-and-fiction television series *The Young Indiana Jones Chronicles*.

THE YOUNG INDIANA JONES CHRONICLES
(novels based on the television series)

YOUNG INDIANA JONES BOOKS
(original novels)

Young Indiana Jones and the . . .

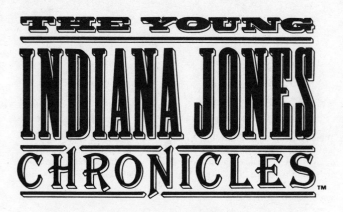

THE YOUNG INDIANA JONES CHRONICLES

Trek of Doom

Adapted by Les Martin

Based on the teleplay "German East Africa,
December 1916"
by Frank Darabont

Story by George Lucas

Directed by Simon Wincer

With photographs from the television show

RANDOM HOUSE 🏠 NEW YORK

This is a work of fiction. While Young Indiana Jones is portrayed as taking part in historical events and meeting real figures from history, many of the characters in the story as well as the situations and scenes have been invented. In addition, where real historical figures and events are described, in some cases the chronology and historical facts have been altered for dramatic effect.

Copyright © 1992 by Lucasfilm Ltd. (LFL)
All rights reserved under International and Pan-American Copyright Conventions. Published in the United States by Random House, Inc., New York, and simultaneously in Canada by Random House of Canada Limited, Toronto.

PHOTO CREDITS: Cover photograph by Brent Petersen, © 1991 by Capital Cities/ABC, Inc. Interior photographs by Keith Hamshere © 1992 Lucasfilm Ltd. Map by Alfred Giuliani.

Library of Congress Cataloging-in-Publication Data
Martin, Les.
   Trek of doom / adapted by Les Martin ; based on the teleplay "German East Africa, December 1916" by Frank Darabont ; story by George Lucas ; directed by Simon Wincer ; with photographs from the television show.
         p. cm. — (Young Indiana Jones chronicles ; TV-5)
   Summary: In December 1916, seventeen-year-old Indiana Jones is a lieutenant in the Belgian Army, fighting the Germans in Africa, and about to embark on a dangerous journey through the uncharted land of the Congo.
   ISBN 0-679-83237-8 (pbk.)
   1. World War, 1914–1916—Campaigns—German East Africa—Juvenile fiction. [1. World War, 1914–1918—Campaigns—German East Africa—Fiction. 2. Zaire—Fiction. 3. Adventure and adventurers—Fiction.] I. Darabont, Frank. II. Lucas, George. III. Title. IV. Series.
PZ7.M36353Tr 1992
[Fic]—dc20 91-51200

Manufactured in the United States of America   10 9 8 7 6 5 4 3 2

Trek of Doom

INDY'S TERRITORY IN "GERMAN

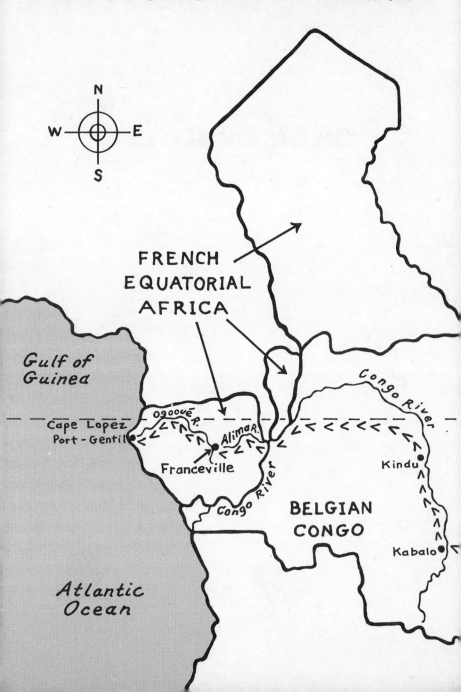

EAST AFRICA, DECEMBER 1916"

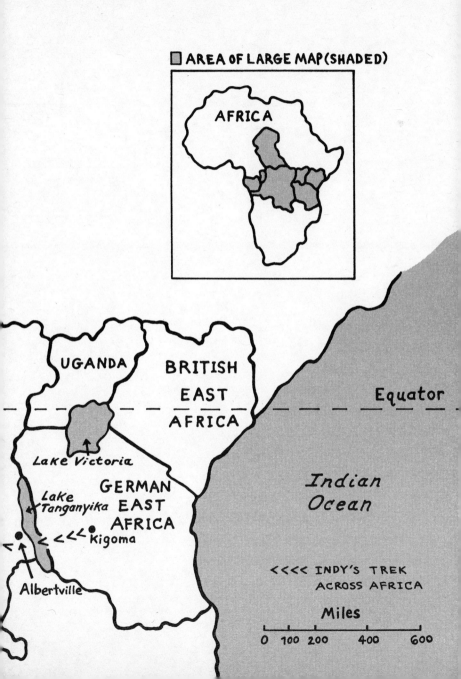

☐ AREA OF LARGE MAP(SHADED)

AFRICA

Equator

UGANDA

BRITISH

EAST

AFRICA

Lake Victoria

GERMAN

Lake
Tanganyika

EAST

AFRICA

Kigoma

Indian
Ocean

Albertville

<<<< INDY'S TREK
ACROSS AFRICA

Miles

0 100 200   400   600

Chapter 1

Major Karl von Regen, of the German Imperial Army, was a bitter man. Instead of fighting for his country in the glorious battles of the Great War in Europe, he had been sent to defend German possessions in Africa. It was like being sent to the moon. No one back home really cared what was happening here. No one would recognize his brilliance and bravery. He would win no medals or promotions. He was a forgotten man in a forgotten war.

But the major was a professional soldier and

a loyal German. He would do his duty as best he could—even with only native Batusi troops whom he despised under his command. Even with a lack of food and medicine and supplies. Even with heat and disease that were as deadly as any human foe.

Now, as he peered through his field glasses at the Belgian forces facing him, he at least had the satisfaction of seeing that the Belgians were as badly off as he. The Belgian troops were native Africans too. He could easily tell that they were askaris because some of them were wearing lion headdresses. As in the German army, only the officers were white. He focused in on one of them. He gave a sardonic smile. The Belgian lieutenant he saw could not have been out of his teens. The Belgians were scraping the bottom of the barrel.

With grim satisfaction, the major watched the young Belgian lining up his squad. Around him other Belgian officers were doing the same. It was clear they were preparing an attack. Well, let them come, the major thought. He had a surprise waiting for them. A deadly surprise. The hardest part of this day's work would be to bury the enemy dead in the African soil after the shooting was over.

• • •

On the other side of the lines, the young Belgian lieutenant squinted at the German barricades. He made sure the askaris under his command were ready to begin their charge as soon as the whistle blew. Then he turned to his friend and fellow lieutenant, Remy Baudouin. "At least it's not as bad as Verdun," Indy Jones said.

"Nothing could be as bad as Verdun," Remy answered, wiping beads of sweat from his forehead and swatting at a fly that had come to rest on his nose.

Both of them fell silent, thinking back to the hell on earth they had left behind in Europe.

They had fought first in the Belgian army in Flanders. Then they were assigned to the French army fighting at Verdun. It was a far cry from what they had expected when they enlisted to fight in the war. Remy had dreamed of heroically defending his native Belgium against the invading Germans. Indy had hoped for a grand adventure. But what they found was gore, not glory—a senseless slaughter that went on and on.

There had been just one way to escape it. They had volunteered to fight in the Belgian campaign to drive the Germans out of Africa.

Indy nodded, remembering. At first it had seemed too good to be true. Not only were they getting out of the nightmare war in Europe, they were actually made officers.

Indy had wondered about that. How did a young soldier like himself rate becoming a lieutenant? In Europe the best he could do was make corporal.

He had asked Remy about it. Remy, who once had been a sailor and had roamed the world, knew the score.

"That's how we do things in Africa," he told Indy. "Almost all our troops in the Belgian Congo are natives, but whites run the show. We give the orders."

Even after a month here, Indy still felt funny about it. It was hard to get used to having men who were bigger, stronger, and older than he was salute him and obey his commands. It didn't seem right. But that was clearly the way things were. From the moment Indy arrived in Africa, he could see that whites ran things the way that they wanted. At least the Belgians did and from what he had seen in the fighting to date, so did the Germans. And he could guess that the English and French had the same system in their possessions, too.

Looking at the enemy barricades and waiting for the signal to attack, Indy said to Remy, "Who'd have thought we'd ever be leading men into battle?"

Remy nodded. "It's strange, all right. I remember being a foot soldier in Europe—and wondering how the officers felt ordering me to put my life on the line. Now I know. It's not such a good feeling."

"But at least it's better out here than back there," Indy said. "Not so much firepower. We don't have to run into a wall of bullets, like at Verdun. The German rifles might pick off some of us—but if the men move fast, zigzag quickly, and keep low, most will get through."

"Yes, we have a fighting chance. That's all a soldier can expect," Remy said. He looked at his watch. Indy did the same. It was almost zero hour. The two of them separated to take up positions in front of the squads of askari troops they led.

Indy glanced back at his men. Their black faces showed no fear. Indy knew he could count on them. They were warriors who had proved themselves many times in battle.

He glanced to his left. He saw Remy loosening the pistol in his belt, ready to lead his men in the charge.

He glanced to his other flank. There, Major Boucher, a hard-bitten professional soldier, had his pistol already out. He had a whistle in his mouth. He had his eyes on his watch. The askari warriors behind him wore traditional lion headdress and had their rifles at the ready. A strange and fierce combination, thought Indy.

Indy pulled his own automatic pistol from its holster. He was leading the spearhead of the charge. He signaled to his men to take aim at the wooden enemy barricade. He raised his hand.

Then, right on time, the whistle blew. Indy swept his hand down. The askaris let off a volley. Bullets splintered the wood of the barricade. There were screams of pain from the enemy.

"*Attaque!*" Indy shouted, charging across the open space. Behind him the roaring askaris followed, eating up the ground, only a handful hit by ragged enemy rifle fire.

On the other side of the barricades, Major von Regen saw panic spreading among his troops. His lips curled in contempt. He barked an order in German to his fellow officer, Lieutenant

Schwinden, who was crouched in a sand-bagged strongpoint.

Schwinden grinned, then whipped off a tarp that covered the German ace in the hole.

A thick-bodied Maxim heavy machine gun.

Schwinden kneeled behind it and opened fire.

A smile spread over von Regen's face as he watched the results.

Bullets cut down askaris like a scythe. The entire charge wave stopped in their tracks and hurled themselves flat against the earth.

Indy hugged the ground as machine gun bullets kicked up dirt five inches from his face.

"A machine gun. God help us," he heard Remy groan from not far away.

Then he heard the commanding voice of Major Boucher shouting, "Fall back! Fall back!"

Indy turned his head. Through a shroud of gunsmoke hanging in the air, he saw Boucher and his men beating a retreat.

Boucher saw Indy and shouted once again, "Lieutenant! I said, fall back!"

Indy heard him. But he heard something else as well.

He heard that the machine gun had fallen silent.

It must have jammed.

That knowledge drove everything else out of Indy's mind.

He only knew that this was their chance. And that they had to take it—fast.

He jumped to his feet and shouted to his men in their native Swahili, "On your feet! Forward! Charge!"

It was at that moment that the sweating, cursing Lieutenant Schwinden got his machine gun working again.

Indy heard its roaring chatter.

Then he felt something like a heavyweight punch on his chest.

A slug had hit him directly over the heart. His brain fogging over, he fell to the ground, and his last thought was, Is this what it feels like to die?

Chapter 2

The fog cleared from Indy's brain. He felt a dull ache in his chest, but his heart was still beating. He was still breathing. He was still alive!

He was surprised. And his surprise was mirrored in the black face bending over him.

The face was that of Sergeant Barthelemy, who had rushed to the aid of his fallen lieutenant, lying facedown in the dust.

Barthelemy rolled Indy over onto his back.

Barthelemy's eyes widened as Indy's eyes opened and met his.

Barthelemy jumped back. Around him the other askaris froze in their headlong retreat when they heard Indy shout, "Fight!"

Indy grabbed his pistol from where it had fallen. He leaped to his feet. His shirt was torn open where the machine gun bullet had hit him. Blood stained the fabric. But his voice was loud and clear. "Come on! I said fight! Fight!"

The askaris knew magic when they saw it. And they knew the power of magic. *Ju-ju,* they called it, and they could see that Indy's *ju-ju* was as strong as it got.

At this moment they would have followed Indy into the jaws of hell. They formed a solid roaring wave as they followed him in a charge at the barricades.

Meanwhile the German machine gun had jammed again. Sweating and cursing, Lieutenant Schwinden struggled to clear it.

At the same time, Remy rallied his askaris and led them to support Indy's attack.

On Indy's other flank, Major Boucher's face turned purple. "Are you deaf, Lieutenant! I said retreat!" he screamed.

But already Boucher's askaris were joining the

charge. Boucher had no choice. He had to charge forward too.

Indy was first over the barricades, with Barthelemy close behind. Behind them poured the askaris, with their bayonets flashing in the sun.

The Batusi soldiers were falling back in disarray, despite Major von Regen's shouts to hold fast. Von Regen emptied his Mauser pistol at the askaris, taking out one with each bullet. Von Regen was a crack shot. By now he had sighted his number one target. Reloading swiftly, he aimed his pistol at the young lieutenant leading the attack.

Too late Indy saw the German major. He braced for the bullet. Only another miracle could save him.

A shot seemed to explode in his ear. He saw the German crumple to the ground.

Indy turned to see Sergeant Barthelemy beside him, holding a smoking rifle.

"Thanks. I owe you—" Indy started to say.

But his thanks were cut off by the loud chatter of the German machine gun. Around Indy, askaris were falling like leaves.

There was no time for Indy to think about what to do. There was just time to do it.

13

He tossed away his pistol and grabbed a rifle from a fallen soldier.

Crouching low and moving fast as a half-back, he came at the sandbagged machine gun position from the side. Without pausing, he hurdled over the sandbags and pulled his rifle trigger when a Batusi rose to meet him with a knife. Suddenly the Batusi wasn't there anymore, blown backward over the sandbags. There was only Lieutenant Schwinden, frantically swinging the machine gun at Indy. Still moving forward, Indy grabbed the searing hot barrel with one hand and pushed it aside. Adrenalin was pouring through him. He barely felt the pain. Or thought about what he was doing, or even felt the impact of metal going into flesh as he bayoneted Schwinden. Still working on pure instinct, Indy shoved aside Schwinden's lifeless body, took control of the machine gun, and turned it on the German forces. His body vibrated as the Maxim thundered.

It took only a few blasts to send the remaining German officers and their Batusi troops in full retreat.

His body trembling, Indy slumped exhausted behind the Maxim.

He could feel the burns on his hand now.

And he could feel slightly sick at the killing he had needed to do.

So this was what victory in battle felt like, he thought. It was a terrible, empty feeling.

Even the sound of the askaris chanting their victory song didn't take away the bitter taste of death.

Listening to the victory chant, Indy wondered why he himself wasn't one of the dead men lying on the ground.

His chest was aching where the machine gun bullet had hit. But his heart was still beating. He looked down at the bullet hole in his shirt. He unbuttoned the top buttons of his shirt and saw where the bullet had gone. It had bashed into the silver locket that he wore dangling from a chain around his neck. A locket with a precious picture in it—a picture of an Austrian princess he had met in Vienna long ago and had never forgotten. He certainly would never forget her now. He pried open the bent locket and saw with relief that the picture was still intact. "Thanks, Princess Sophie," he said softly.

Suddenly he stiffened.

He heard a voice behind him. The voice blazed with fury above the askaris' chants.

"Lieutenant! I'm going to get you for this!"

Indy turned to face his superior officer, Major Boucher.

Indy had another kind of sick feeling.

One battle might be over—but a new one had just begun.

Indy faced Major Boucher's full fire back at headquarters late that afternoon.

He was ordered to the tent of Colonel Mathieu, commander of this front. Remy was summoned, too, as a witness.

There was no mercy in Major Boucher's voice as he grilled Indy. "You *did* hear my order to retreat, Lieutenant?"

"Yes, sir," Indy admitted, standing stiffly at attention, eyes front, only his lips moving.

"Yet you chose to disobey," Boucher went on.

"The German machine gun jammed. I saw an opportunity to advance," Indy explained.

Boucher would have none of it. "In defiance of a superior officer. Isn't that right?" He shoved his face close to Indy's. "What was that, Lieutenant? I didn't hear you! Speak up!"

"Yes, sir! In defiance of a superior officer!" Indy said.

"If that machine gun had unjammed before you reached the barricades, the entire company would have been wiped out." Boucher pressed his point home.

Indy opened his mouth, but could think of nothing to say.

Colonel Mathieu cleared his throat loudly in the silence.

All eyes turned to him.

"Major Boucher, you have the right to press charges if you wish," the colonel said. "But be advised that I've received a message from General Tombeur. Today's action broke the back of German defenses here. The general is very pleased. He's awarded us a company citation. And he's given the young lieutenant here a promotion."

Boucher stiffened, as if someone had rammed a poker down his spine. "I see," he said shortly.

"It would be a shame to stain our victory with controversy, don't you think?" the colonel went on smoothly, giving Boucher a pointed look.

Boucher nodded with the jerky motion of a puppet whose strings were being pulled.

"Yes, I suppose it would," he said.

The colonel smiled. "Then that's that. Now to more pleasant matters." He went to Indy and pinned a captain's insignia on Indy's collar. "By order of General Tombeur, with his thanks. Congratulations—*Captain*."

"Thank you, sir!" Indy said, swelling with pride as he saluted.

Then the colonel got back to business—the business of war.

He went to where the captured German Maxim stood. He patted it fondly. "Here's the real prize," he said. "Worth its weight in gold. Months ago we were promised a shipment of arms like this from Europe, but the weapons never arrived. Until now."

Everyone in the tent perked up his ears. This was news. Big news. In the battle for Africa, it took only a few heavy weapons to turn the tide of battle. Too often the Germans had most of them.

The colonel moved to a map of Africa on the tent wall. The others gathered around him. His finger tapped the map at the heart of the continent. "This is where we are." His finger traced a route from Europe down around the southern tip of Africa at the Cape of Good Hope and then up to a port on the east coast. "The shipment was supposed to land here, at Chinde. There is an excellent supply route from there to our location. But the ship ran aground on the west coast at Cape Lopez. Our weapons are gathering dust at the French garrison at Port-Gentil. Two dozen Vickers machine guns, four mortars, and two light British howitzers."

Remy gave a low whistle.

"Imagine what we could do with those," Indy said, just as impressed.

"Especially when we try to take the German fort at Tabora," Remy said. "I don't fancy going up against their seventy-sevens with nothing but our rifles and our sweet dispositions."

Colonel Mathieu beamed. "I'm glad you see it that way. Because I am assigning you and our new captain here to serve on an expedition to get those weapons."

Remy's mouth dropped open. "An expedition? Across the Congo?"

Colonel Mathieu nodded. "Yes, it should be quite simple. You leave tomorrow."

Remy said nothing. There was nothing to say. The colonel had given an order.

The most Remy could do was exchange a glance with Indy. Indy could see in Remy's eyes just what Remy thought about this mission.

It was simple, no doubt about it.

Simple suicide.

Chapter 3

Indy had an uneasy feeling as he watched Colonel Mathieu slowly move his finger over a map of Africa.

Indy remembered the French brass at the battle of Verdun. He remembered how they had moved their fingers over their maps of the battlefield.

It was so easy for a commander to move his finger a few inches on a map. But thousands upon thousands of soldiers had died at Verdun trying to move across those few inches.

Now Colonel Mathieu's finger easily moved across Africa from east to west. He was showing the officers the route of their march. Its starting point was their current position, pressing into German East Africa. It moved over the width of the Belgian Congo, carved out of the heart of Africa. It then moved into French Equatorial Africa, on the western border of the Belgian colony. It finally arrived at Port-Gentil, on the west coast of the continent.

"The journey should be no problem," the colonel said confidently. "An easy march over the highlands. A boat trip across Lake Tanganyika. From there you can take the railway to the Congo River, where you will be able to take a river steamer to Bonga. You will then proceed on foot to Franceville, on the Ogooué River, where you will pick up a boat to Port-Gentil. Anyone have any questions?"

Indy was slightly surprised to see Major Boucher step forward. On second thought, though, he shouldn't have been. Indy didn't much like the major, but he had to respect him. The man was no armchair commander. He was a front line officer, a professional who knew his business down to the last nitty-gritty detail.

Boucher had one detail on his mind now. A very big detail.

"You say we go from Bonga to Franceville on foot," he said. "Wouldn't it be better to take the Congo to the west coast, and then take a boat up the coast to Port-Gentil?"

Colonel Mathieu gave a short cough. "Unfortunately, there's been a little . . . native unrest along that route. German agents are suspected of stirring up the population. We'll have it cleared up soon, but for the time being it's best we stay out of the area."

"Bad luck," said Boucher, grimly studying the map.

"The march from Bonga to Franceville—you have a problem with that?" said the colonel, raising his eyebrows.

"The march is possible—but hardly ideal," the major said. "The terrain is merciless. We can expect to lose a lot of men. What about the French? Can't they ship the weapons to us?"

"They haven't the transportation to spare," the colonel replied.

"What about the British?" asked Boucher. "They have the ships, surely, to take the weapons around the Cape."

"Our commanding general prefers not to seek

British help," the colonel replied stiffly. "The British already have enough influence in Africa, and even now they are preparing to add the German territory they conquer to their empire. We Belgians must do our own fighting. If we take British help, we will have to take British orders, and we will wind up giving them our spoils of war. We must remember, Major, that we are not fighting here so that the British flag should fly over land won by our blood."

Major Boucher nodded. He was a Belgian soldier and patriot through and through. "I understand," he said.

"Any more questions?" the colonel asked the group.

There were none.

"Have a good dinner, and get a good night's sleep, gentlemen," the colonel said. "It will be your last civilized meal and night in a bed for some time."

Indy turned to Remy. "Wait outside for me. I want to talk to the colonel a minute."

As the others left, Indy approached Mathieu. "Colonel, may I have a word?"

"Of course, *Captain*," Mathieu said, smiling.

"First, I want to thank you for my promotion," Indy began.

"You earned it," the colonel said.

"I doubt that Major Boucher sees it that way," Indy said, getting to his question. "With all respect, sir, I was wondering why you've chosen to put us together on this journey. There might be some—friction."

"There may be friction, but there will also be the kind of chemistry I want," the colonel explained. "The major is a careful soldier. Very disciplined. Used to making hard decisions. These are qualities you would do well to learn."

Indy nodded, and the colonel continued. "On the other hand, as you may have observed, the major tends to be a bit cautious and inflexible. He needs some of your daring, some of your imagination. I expect you to give him your support. Between the two of you, I think we stand an excellent chance of getting those guns."

"You can depend on us, sir," Indy assured him.

"Captain, I'm depending on *you,*" the colonel declared. "I know my faith is not misplaced."

Indy felt his chest swell with pride. He gave the colonel a razor-sharp salute. "No, sir! I won't let you down!"

When Indy got outside, though, he still had to deal with Remy's doubts.

"Lord, a trek across Africa," Remy said. "What idiot thought this one up?"

Indy grinned. "Just think of it as a little hike."

"A hike, he says." Remy grimaced. "I'd rather be back in the trenches than go through that jungle. We got a good look at it when we sailed up the Congo to join the troops here. It looked like a green hell."

"Look, the askaris don't seem worried about it—and they know this land better than we do," Indy said as they approached a bonfire that the troops had started. The men were celebrating their victory with dancing and drums. When they saw Indy, they turned toward him in unison and chanted, *"Mungo-kidogo!"*

"What's that mean?" Remy wondered.

"Mungo-kidogo," said Indy, wrinkling his brows. His command of the askari languages was limited. Sergeant Barthelemy had come up to greet him. *"Mungo-kidogo . . .* little god?" Indy asked him, puzzled.

Barthelemy flashed a smile. "Askari soldiers see you struck down by bad German bullet, Captain. They see you die—and come back to

25

life." Barthelemy pretended to spit. "They see you cough up bullet, spit on ground with much contempt. Then you lead askari to victory! Very big magic."

"No, Barthelemy. The men have it wrong. It's not magic," Indy told him. "I'm just lucky." Indy pulled out the locket that the bullet had bashed into. "The bullet struck my locket, see?"

By now the askaris had gathered around them. The sight of the locket made them murmur with awe.

"This *very* small target," Barthelemy said. "Your *ju-ju* very powerful. *Mungo-kidogo!* Little god! He who cannot die!"

At these words the askaris cheered again, while Remy shook his head.

"Two promotions in one day, Indy," Remy commented. "First captain, now god."

Remy wasn't the only one to look askance at Indy's exploits. That night Major Boucher came to Indy and Remy's tent to make his own feelings clear.

"Congratulations, *Captain*," he told Indy.

"Thank you, sir," Indy responded instantly.

"On coming close to getting us all killed!" Boucher went on, his voice rising to a shout.

Indy froze, as did Remy beside him.

Boucher looked at the new captain with clear contempt. That same contempt was in his voice. "What you did today was hardly cause for promotion. It was stupid. The next time you disobey my command, I'll skin you alive and feed you to the hyenas. Do I make myself clear?"

"As a bell, sir," Indy choked out.

Boucher looked coldly at the dented locket lying on Indy's bunk. "You have the devil's luck. I hope it holds. We can all use some of it on this trip."

With that the major gave them a salute, waited for them to return it, and left the tent.

"Not a guy to make your enemy," Remy said, shaking his head.

"He'll run us into the ground," Indy agreed. "With him in charge, who needs the Germans?"

"Fortunately, we've got no worries," Remy said dryly. "Not with your *ju-ju*." Remy lay down on his bunk and lowered his mosquito netting. "Good night, mango-gorgonzola—or whatever your name is nowadays."

Indy was left sitting on his bunk with his locket in his hand. He pried it open and looked at the small photo in the bent frame.

It was of a girl Indy had met when he was just leaving childhood behind. Sophie was the daughter of the Austrian archduke Franz Ferdinand. She was the first girl to make Indy's heart beat faster. She had shown him how beautiful and brave a girl could be, in an adventure in Vienna before the war.

How far away all that seemed now. Indy wondered if he would ever see Sophie again. Or a world at peace. Or even if he would get out of Africa alive.

He'd just have to play it day by day, and danger by danger. In this war that showed no sign of ending. And on this journey that seemed to stretch beyond the horizon of hope.

Chapter 4

They lined up to march out of camp at dawn the next day. The officers in charge of the trek stood in a group at the head of the column of soldiers. Major Boucher. Captain LaFleur, the medical officer. A young lieutenant named Arnaud. Remy and Indy.

Five officers, thought Indy, all of them non-African. He looked back at their command. Sergeant Barthelemy was going up and down the column, prodding the men to straighten up their gear and straighten out their line. Thirty-five of them, all natives. Behind them were fifty native bearers to haul supplies.

Indy heard Boucher's voice in his ear.

"You may give the order to march, Captain," Boucher said.

"For-waaard!" Indy bellowed at the top of his lungs.

The officers, accompanied by two native guides, moved out first. Behind them came the troops and the bearers, who were chanting rhythmically as if the song might lighten their heavy loads.

Other askari troops stopped their morning activities to watch them go. Many waved farewell. There were wives and children in camp as well, despite all official orders. More than a few were wailing and crying as their husbands and fathers marched off.

The column marched past Colonel Mathieu, who had come out to review the troops and see them off. "Godspeed, gentlemen," he said, snapping the officers a salute.

The officers returned it. As they did, Indy heard Major Boucher mutter beside him, "We could do with fewer good wishes and more bearers. We'll be short of everything from bullets to bandages. And to feed ourselves we'll have to live off the land."

"You mean, hunt game?" asked Indy. Already he could feel himself swinging into the rhythm of the march as he and Boucher talked. And already he could feel the heat from the rising sun on the back of his neck. By noon it would feel like a blast furnace.

"Hardly," said Boucher. "This is not a hunting expedition. We will have to get food from the villages on our way."

"What if they don't want to give us any?" asked Indy. "They might be short themselves. This war must have fouled up the native economy."

"They won't have any choice," Boucher replied with a shrug. "We will order them to, in the name of the Belgian government. The natives will not refuse. They will not dare to."

"But there are so many of them, and so few of us," Indy commented.

"Numbers do not matter. Willpower does. Willpower—and firepower," Boucher said. "We Belgians rule the Congo because we have both."

"But what if the natives get ahold of guns of their own?" Indy wondered aloud. "What if they decide to make their own decisions about what they do and don't do?"

Boucher snorted. "As I suspected, you are a dreamer, Captain. You think that these people can actually rule themselves. Or even want to."

"The thought has crossed my mind," Indy admitted. "I mean, what are they fighting this war for? When it's over, they're going to expect their reward. After all, that's the difference between our side and the Germans, right? *They're* the ones who believe that people should just follow orders. *We're* the ones who believe in democracy."

"That's in Europe—this is Africa," the major replied. He talked to Indy as a kindergarten teacher would talk to a pupil. "I assure you, these natives are like children. They have to be told what to do—and punished if they break the rules."

"Belgian rules," said Indy.

"Belgian rules," agreed Boucher.

By now the camp was out of sight. The rolling highland plain—the veld—stretched empty around them from horizon to horizon. Above them the sky was pure unbroken blue. Indy felt immeasurably tiny. He felt as if he and the others were ants crawling over this vastness.

He took out a handkerchief and mopped his forehead as he marched. He didn't like to think of what the soldiers felt like, with their heavy rifles and full field packs. And the bearers with their backbreaking loads.

And this was only the beginning.

Even after they marched over the veld, more than a thousand miles of lake, river, and jungle lay ahead of them.

Indy couldn't imagine that kind of distance.

But somehow he and the others would have to cover it—the same way that once upon a time in America pioneers had to cross deserts and mountains, and battle nature and natives, to reach their goal.

The old pioneer spirit, he told himself, that's what he'd need.

Suddenly he heard Major Boucher's voice shouting, "Sergeant Barthelemy, get your men moving! This is no stroll through the country-side! We cover forty-five kilometers before sunset—or else they get no food. Unless they want to eat each other!"

Indy looked back at Barthelemy. The big sergeant's face showed no expression. What did Barthelemy think about this march? About this war? What kind of spirit did Barthelemy and the other askaris have? Certainly not a pioneer spirit. This was Africa, not America. This was their land and the land of their ancestors, from before the dawn of history.

"What was that business about them eating each other?" he asked Boucher. "You know as well as I do that the askaris aren't cannibals. From what I've heard since I got here, practically no Africans are."

"You still don't understand how to treat the native troops," Boucher said. "They must be kept in their place. They must be reminded that they are little more than savages, and that they are serving a superior race. They have to feel that they are being honored by wearing our uniform and serving under our flag."

Indy thought of Barthelemy marching behind them. Barthelemy was as good a sergeant and fighting man as Indy had seen anywhere. He was strong, brave, intelligent, resourceful. Indy wondered how grateful and honored Barthelemy was to be treated like a child or a dumb animal.

Maybe he, Indy, could talk to Barthelemy sometime and find out. But almost instantly Indy realized how slim the chances of that were. In the army it was hard enough for officers to have friendly conversations with men in the ranks. There was always a barrier of rank between them. And here in Africa the barrier was even higher—a barrier between white and black that few, if any, could get past.

Still, Indy thought, he'd like to try. Maybe sometime on this trek he'd get a chance. He'd stay alert for it.

At that moment he heard Barthelemy's voice. "Sir! Majuh! We must stop."

Boucher whirled around. The officers with him did the same.

"What is it, Sergeant?" Boucher demanded impatiently, glancing at his wristwatch even as he spoke. "Make it fast—we have to keep on schedule. A steamer is waiting for us at Lake Tanganyika."

"A bearer—he fall down," Barthelemy said. "Sick."

"Check him out, LaFleur—quickly," Boucher commanded.

"Yes, sir," the medical officer said, and hurried to where one of the native bearers lay on the ground.

Minutes later LaFleur returned. "He has the sweats and shakes. Malaria. He needs rest. And quinine pills."

Boucher shrugged. "We have no time to rest. And what is our supply of quinine?"

LaFleur grimaced. "Not as much as I would like. We have just about enough to last us through the trip—if we are careful."

"Then we can't waste any on bearers," Boucher decided. "We can always hire new ones. Make sure to give all officers one quinine pill a day. The askaris can get one every two days—or every three or four days if we start running short."

Boucher turned to Barthelemy, who was standing at attention within earshot and awaiting orders. "Leave the man here with a little food and water. He'll have to make it back to camp the best he can. Split his load among the other bearers."

"But, sir—" Barthelemy began.

"This is an order," Boucher said in an icy tone. "We've wasted enough time already."

"Yes, sir," Barthelemy said in a voice that betrayed no emotion. He saluted and went to carry out the order.

"I hope you take this as a lesson," Boucher said to Indy. "As an officer, you must never waver in your command. Strength and certainty are the only things these people will respect."

"But the bearer—" Indy said.

"Don't be sentimental," Boucher said. "On any mission there are necessary losses."

"Anyway, this fellow was lucky," Remy commented. "He stands a good chance of getting back okay. We're just a half a day out of camp. And these bearers are tough."

Lieutenant Arnaud saw the look on Indy's face and put his hand on Indy's shoulder. "You'll have to get used to it. This won't be the only case of sickness you'll see on this trip."

Captain LaFleur agreed. "This is different from the war in Europe. Here the big killer isn't enemy fire. It's disease. Malaria. Yellow fever. Sleeping sickness. Parasites. That's just to mention a few that we have names for. Plus others that we discover only when men die from them."

"Exactly," Major Boucher said with satisfaction. "That's why we must establish a policy now on how we treat the sick—and stick to it. Otherwise we don't stand a chance of ever reaching Port-Gentil." He stared hard at Indy. "I hope you agree, *Captain*."

At this moment Indy's captain's bars felt heavy as lead on his tunic. With an effort, he stiffened himself up. "Yes, sir," he said.

"Then give the order to march," Boucher said.

"For-waaard!" Indy bellowed.

But not as loudly as before.

Chapter 5

On the march across the veld, and on the voyage across Lake Tanganyika, Indy began to fully understand how beautiful Africa was. On the highlands of the veld vast grasslands spread from horizon to horizon, broken only by stands of graceful trees and shimmering streams. Gazelles sped away at the sound of the soldiers' marching feet, hooves seeming to barely touch the ground. Herds of zebras galloped past. Now and then Indy spied lions lying lazily in the tall grass, resting after a kill, or beginning to stir as hunger spurred them to go on another hunt.

There was game everywhere. Indy thought again of the American West, before hunters with rapid-fire rifles, and farmers with plows, and ranchers with barbed wire, and railway workers with sledgehammers and spikes came to tame it. On the steamer, as Indy looked out at the pure, sparkling water of Tanganyika, all war and battle, pain and suffering, seemed a million miles away. It was like sailing over the top of the world.

But Indy also began to understand how merciless Africa was.

By the time the expedition reached Kigoma on the east shore of Lake Tanganyika, almost a quarter of the bearers had been left behind. Those remaining said nothing about the extra load they had to carry. Instead they made their feelings known by simply disappearing during the night before the steamer sailed.

At this Major Boucher merely shrugged. "Typical," he said. "Only to be expected. They didn't even wait for their pay."

"There wasn't much to wait for," was Indy's comment. "I can't believe that people would work so hard for so little."

"That's because you don't know the natives," said Boucher. "They are only too happy to work for practically nothing."

"Then you don't think their leaving us cold has anything to do with low wages?" Indy asked dryly.

"Not at all," Boucher said. "They're simply irresponsible, like children. But no matter. We can hire more when we dock on the western shore of the lake, at Albertville."

He was right. Native bearers swarmed around the docks at Albertville. But by the time the expedition reached the railway at Kabalo, almost a fifth of them had fallen sick. And when the expedition got off the creaking, slow-moving train at the Congo River port of Kindu, there was no room for the remaining bearers on the river steamboat going north to Bonga.

Again Boucher was unconcerned. "We'll pick up more bearers when we arrive there. In Africa there is no shortage of cheap labor."

Again he was right. At the Bonga docks, native laborers lined up, eager for work.

Boucher smiled at Indy. "You see, these people will work for whatever we choose to give them. It is better than what they now have—which is nothing."

"But what did they do for money before Belgium took control here?" Indy wondered.

"They had their own primitive culture, I suppose," said Boucher. "Did a lot of bartering, traded cattle and such. But that is long gone. We have taught them to want and need our goods. And taught them, too, that they need money to pay for them. They are only too eager to earn whatever they can get."

Indy grimaced. "It's better than making them slaves, I guess."

"What an idea," Boucher said indignantly. "Belgium is a civilized nation."

Lieutenant Arnaud, who had been listening, chimed in, "That's why our country took over the Congo. For many years our former king, Leopold, claimed it as his personal property. And he had nothing against slavery. It was only when word leaked out about what he was doing to the natives that public opinion forced him to turn the Congo over to Belgium."

"Since then we have been introducing the natives to the benefits of civilization," Boucher concluded with satisfaction. "We are performing a splendid service for them. They owe us a great debt."

Indy thought of the native bearers sweating

under their loads. He thought of the askari soldiers putting their lives on the line. Belgium seemed to be collecting that debt in full—and with interest.

"So when do you think the people here will be civilized enough to run their own country?" Indy asked.

Boucher's face hardened. "This is not *their* country. It is Belgium's. *To say anything else is treason.*"

Indy decided to drop the subject. Anything more he had to say would just get him into trouble. And more trouble with Boucher was not what he needed. The toughest territory of the trek still lay ahead. They would have to work as a team if they hoped to make it to Port-Gentil.

At that moment Captain LaFleur arrived with fresh news.

"Two of the askaris are running high fevers," the medical officer reported.

"The cause?" demanded Boucher.

"Can't say for sure," LaFleur said. "Blackwater fever, perhaps. Or cholera. Malaria, maybe, since we had to cut their quinine after half our supply was stolen by a bearer."

"It doesn't really matter what it is," Boucher decided. "We'll leave them behind here at

Bonga. We can't have any sick men slowing us down. Is there a hospital here?"

"Something called a hospital—run by missionaries," LaFleur reported.

"It's better than what the men would find in the jungle we're heading into," Boucher declared.

"You don't mean you'd leave sick men behind in the jungle?" Indy said. "I mean, they're *our* men. We have a responsibility toward them."

"The only responsibility we have is toward our mission," Boucher said sternly. "This is war. And in war, a soldier's duty is to die."

A shiver ran through Indy. He remembered hearing a French general say virtually those same words at the battle of Verdun.

Verdun might be far away. Europe might be far away. But war was still war, wherever it was fought.

Here, though, the enemy was different. But just as deadly.

Disease.

It lived in the air, the water, the food. The very soil beneath their feet. Disease gave no warning—and mocked all defenses.

Before LaFleur left to take the soldiers to the

primitive hospital, he commented, "These are typical casualties. We lose dozens of men to sickness for every one hit by a German bullet. As for me, I'd rather face bullets than what we're going up against."

Those grim words kept echoing through Indy's mind as the expedition left Bonga and moved into the jungle. The jungle spread like a blanket from the Belgian Congo over French Equatorial Africa.

Indy saw native bearers collapse and be left behind, moaning, weeping, and pleading.

He saw askaris sweating with fever, being supported by their fellow soldiers so that they did not slow the pace of the march.

He saw supplies of medicine dwindle, and saw Captain LaFleur's face become etched with helpless despair.

He saw Boucher snarl more and more harshly at the troops. And saw Barthelemy labor harder and harder to keep them in some kind of order as the expedition moved deeper and deeper into the jungle. Painfully they followed almost invisible trails through thick forests and over rushing, swirling streams. Uphill and downhill. Through steambath heat and drenching rain. Through clouds of insects swarming in the men's faces. Meanwhile, deadly snakes slid close to their feet and curled in branches overhead. The yellow eyes of leopards watched warily from the bushes as the men filed by.

Each night Indy watched an ever more discouraged Boucher shaking his head. He marked their pitiful progress on a map before it was time to try to sleep draped in mosquito netting.

Each dawn when Indy awoke he first quickly checked himself. Then he looked closely at those around him for signs of sickness. Next it was time to find out what shape the askaris were in. And then how many bearers had deserted in the dark.

He could not forget LaFleur's prophetic words even had he wanted to—especially after seeing the Ubangi village that the expedition entered looking for food and fresh bearers.

Indy never learned the name of the village, but he had his own name for it.

The Village of the Dead.

Chapter 6

They had emerged from the jungle to reach a broad stretch of highlands. They should have been able to move faster now, but hunger slowed them. And the handful of remaining bearers were badly overloaded.

As they moved along a ridgeline, they spotted the village in the broad valley below.

"At last a piece of good luck," said Lieutenant Arnaud, wiping his face with a sweat-stained handkerchief. "We'll be able to get food there. And hire more bearers."

But Major Boucher held up his hand, bringing the column to a halt.

"Not so fast," he said. He focused his binoculars on the village. "There's something about this place I don't like. The natives should have noticed us by now. Somehow they always know when there are strangers near. They should be coming out of their huts to gawk at us and try to sell us anything they have. But I don't see a soul. For some reason, they're all keeping out of sight."

"German troops there, you think?" asked Indy.

Boucher shook his head. "Not likely. Not this far west. Though I don't rule out German agents, come to stir up the natives. But more likely it's deserters. Scum who have fled our service. We'll have to proceed with caution. They might be armed. Tell the men."

Indy commanded the askaris, "Rifles at the ready. Advance."

With the officers leading the way with pistols in their hands, and the bearers staying well behind, the troops cautiously entered the village and fanned out.

Still there was no one to be seen.

But there was a smell in the air. A smell

that made Indy's stomach do a slow roll-over.

"Ugh," Remy said, wrinkling his nose with disgust. "What is that stink?"

Barthelemy, moving beside Remy and Indy, said, "Dis a bad place, Cap'n."

At that moment there was a shout from one of the askaris. Lieutenant Arnaud hurried to investigate.

"Major!" he shouted. "There's a body over here!"

Everyone headed to where Arnaud and the askaris stood looking down.

"My God," said Indy, following their gaze.

The corpse of a native, hideously swollen, lay half-hidden in the grass. Huge black flies buzzed around the decaying flesh.

Major Boucher's expression didn't change. "Check the huts," he ordered in a clipped voice.

Indy and Remy were the first to obey. They opened the flap of the nearest hut. It took their eyes a moment to adjust to the dim light.

"Sweet Jesus," Remy said.

The floor of the hut was carpeted with corpses, stiff and swollen, twisted in final agony. At the sudden light, a cloud of flies rose angrily into the air.

Indy let the flap fall shut.

"What the devil happened here?" Boucher demanded of Captain LaFleur.

"Smallpox, from the look of it," LaFleur replied.

"Smallpox? The entire *village?*" Indy said, unable to believe the horror.

"Our program of vaccination is on the drawing board," said LaFleur. "It was delayed by the war."

"Order the men to move out of here—fast," Boucher cut in.

"They won't need any urging," said Remy. "They look like they're about to turn and run. Can't say I blame them."

Suddenly they heard Barthelemy's voice shouting, "Majuh! Majuh! Come quickly."

The askaris and the officers headed for him on the run, guns at the ready.

When they saw what he had found, they lowered their weapons.

A small native boy, somewhere between three and four years old, painfully thin and dirty, squatted in the dust beside the corpse of an old man. Silently the little boy stared at the strangers.

"Seems we've found a survivor," Remy said.

The soldiers watched, torn between pity and awe, as the little boy went back to what he had been doing. He dripped cool water from a soaked cloth onto the old man's chest. Then he stood up and toddled to a nearby stream to soak the cloth again.

It was only then that the soldiers could see he was tied to the old man by a rawhide tether wrapped around his ankle like a leash.

"What's he doing?" asked Indy.

"He was left to care for the old man," LaFleur said.

"Poor thing," said Indy. He squatted beside the boy and wiggled his fingers. "Hey, little fella."

Barthelemy squatted beside Indy, and reached out to untie the child.

Major Boucher's voice cut through the air like a whiplash. "Don't touch him. He's diseased."

Barthelemy looked puzzled. "Majuh . . . if we cannot touch chil', how we take him wid us?"

"We don't, Sergeant," Boucher responded icily. "We leave him right where he is."

Indy rose to his feet. "But, sir . . . he's just a little boy," he said in a stunned voice.

"Yes? And?" Boucher said with a tinge of contempt.

"He can't care for himself," Indy protested. "If we leave him here, he'll die."

"He's as good as dead already, Captain," Boucher stated flatly. "I won't have him brought along as a sentimental gesture to spread sickness among the men."

"Sir, I disagree," Indy said, a flicker of anger lighting his eyes.

Boucher leaned toward him, his face hard. "You're being irrational. Letting your emotions cloud your judgment. A good officer must learn that one bad decision can endanger his men and put his entire command at risk."

"Yes, sir," Indy said, biting his lip. He would have liked to argue more, but he knew Boucher was right—in a way. A way that Indy had to swallow like a bitter pill. He had a hard time stomaching it, though.

"A rational decision, Captain," Boucher said approvingly. "You must always remember our mission." He turned to Remy and Arnaud. "Have the men form up. We move out in two minutes."

Boucher strode off with the others, leaving Indy alone with Barthelemy and the child.

"You leave boy behin', Cap'n Indy?" Barthelemy demanded.

Indy avoided Barthelemy's gaze. "I'm not in command," he said. It was not easy to get the words out.

"Dis a Ubangi chil'," Barthelemy said. "Ubangi, like me. Barthelemy t'ink you would not leave chil' behin' . . . if dis was a *white* chil'."

Indy opened his mouth to talk the matter out. He hadn't known that Barthelemy was Ubangi. He could see how that might make a difference.

Then he stiffened. What difference did it make? He was a captain, Barthelemy was a sergeant, and this was the army.

"Orders are orders," Indy forced himself to say. "Gather the men."

And he walked off after the other officers without looking back.

There was no looking back on this mission, he told himself.

Not with what lay ahead of them on the next leg of this trek.

They were going back into the jungle. By now Indy knew the jungle well enough to know the law that governed it. Only the fittest survived the jungle. And the price of weakness was . . . death.

Chapter 7

Indy swung his razor-sharp machete as hard as he could at the enemy.

The enemy was the jungle.

For days now everyone on the expedition had been taking turns hacking through the dense foliage to blaze a trail for the slowly moving column of men and supplies. Today it was Indy's and Remy's turn to slash at the vegetation that seemed to stretch out forever before them.

"My arm's going to fall off," groaned Remy

as his machete swished through the air. "Will we ever get out of here?"

"We won't if we give up," grunted Indy in reply, not pausing in his rhythm. Sweat was draining out of every pore. He no longer noticed it. He had almost forgotten what it was like to have dry skin and clean clothing. He could barely imagine that there was a world where people took baths and slept between cool sheets. All that there was in his world now was stifling heat and gloomy dim light. Buzzing insects and shrieking birds. Leafy branches that slapped in your face, and vines that curled around your feet. Tall flowering plants that seemed to grab at your arms. All that was in his mind was the machete getting heavier and heavier in his hand and blisters on his palm opening up and Boucher's voice from behind rasping in his ears, "Keep up the pace! We have ten kilometers to go before dark!"

"Hey, hear that?" Remy said, freezing.

From the darkness of the jungle came an angry snarl.

Indy shrugged, and swung his machete. "Just a big pussycat."

"Yeah, a big pussycat with a big appetite," said Remy, getting back to work.

Suddenly a figure came staggering up beside them. It was one of the askaris. He was moving unsteadily, like a runner who had run himself out. He was panting desperately, gasping for air. There was a thick sheen of sweat on his face. His eyes were bulging, like those of a fish deep underwater. He was reeling, trying to keep his balance. Then, while Indy and Remy watched helplessly, he collapsed. He lay violently shivering on the jungle floor.

"Lieutenant! Captain! Keep walking!" shouted Major Boucher as he came forward with Arnaud and LaFleur to check out the situation.

But Indy was already kneeling. He put his hand on the man's forehead. "My God. He's burning up."

LaFleur kneeled beside Indy. He examined the man.

"Smallpox?" asked Boucher anxiously.

LaFleur shook his head. "Yellow fever. It's bad."

"Is it contagious?" asked Boucher. "Can he give it to anyone else?"

"No," said LaFleur.

"Thank God," said Boucher.

"But that doesn't matter," said LaFleur grimly. "The disease is carried by mosquitoes—and I don't have to tell you that there's no escape from them here."

"Then you think there are more cases," said Boucher.

LaFleur nodded. "I've spotted a few early signs among the men—and the disease comes on fast. This victim is just the first. From now on, they'll start dropping in their tracks as this man did."

"Pardon me, sir," Indy said. "I'll go get the men to rig up a stretcher. It shouldn't take long."

Boucher gave him a puzzled look. "A stretcher?"

"Yes, sir, a stretcher," Indy said, already knowing what was coming.

"What do you think we need a stretcher for?" Boucher inquired, raising his eyebrows.

"Why, to carry this sick man, sir," Indy said, trying to keep his voice calm. It was always a mistake to show feeling in front of Boucher.

The major's mouth curled with contempt. "I was hoping this trip would have made an officer of you by now. I told you at the very start that we can afford to let nothing slow us down. Nothing."

"Yes, sir," Indy said. "But—"

"*But* you have refused to listen," said

Boucher. "Well, listen now. Any man who cannot keep up with us on his own feet will be left behind. *Do I make myself clear?*"

"But they'll be eaten by beasts," Indy protested.

"What do you want us to do—carry them on our backs?" asked Boucher sarcastically.

"If it comes to that," Indy insisted.

"We can't make it through this jungle burdened by the sick," said Boucher. "If the healthy and the sick stick together, they die together." He turned to LaFleur. "Provide anyone who falls out with minimum rations. And make sure they know the direction back to Bonga. Who knows, perhaps some of them may make it."

"Yeah—and the sun might rise in the west tomorrow," said Indy.

"We will also leave them their guns with a few rounds," Boucher went on, ignoring Indy. "They can protect themselves from those beasts that the young captain here seems so worried about."

LaFleur nodded. "Either that—or they can shorten their own suffering."

Indy demanded to be heard. "First a child, then our own men. Whom do we leave behind next, *Major?*"

"Whomever reason dictates, *Captain*," responded Boucher.

LaFleur put a sympathetic hand on Indy's shoulder. "It's painful, I know. Just think of it as leaving our dead behind."

Indy looked at the shivering askari's sweating face, his bulging eyes. He thought of the other askaris he had seen having a hard time keeping up with even the slow progress they were making. Stumbling. Shivering. Sweating, with eyes bulging. Seven or eight at least.

Not for the first time he remembered what the name Boucher meant in English.

Butcher.

He stood still, facing Boucher. "It's hard to think of them as 'our dead.' Real hard. When their eyes are still alive to accuse us."

Boucher didn't even blink. His voice was dry as dust. "Now, if you have nothing more on your mind, Captain, you can continue with your task," he commanded.

Indy stood still a moment longer. He had said, "Yes, sir," when the major had ordered the first bearer left behind on the veld. He had said, "Yes, sir," when the major had ordered the child left behind in the village. He wondered how long he could keep on saying "Yes, sir," when each time it made his stomach turn a little more.

"Well, Captain, let's get on with it," said Boucher, his voice growing sharper.

Indy swallowed hard. "Yes, sir," he said. He could barely manage to get the words out. He stooped and picked up his machete. It seemed even heavier. Then he turned and began hacking viciously at the jungle again, not looking back.

"Charge!" Indy leads an attack on the Germans, ignoring Major Boucher's orders.

Sergeant Barthelemy *(left)* and Remy *(center)* admire
the locket that stopped a bullet and saved Indy's life.

The men begin their trek across Africa.

Colonel Mathieu *(center)* traces the route that Major Boucher *(left)*, Remy, and Indy will take through the Congo.

Everyone is surprised when Barthelemy discovers an Ubangi child, the only survivor from a village wiped out by smallpox.

Remy and Indy discover that they are much deeper in the jungle than Major Boucher told them.

Indy forces an irrational Major Boucher to drop his gun.

The hidden enemy—disease—claims the lives of many soldiers.

Indy writes in his journal while the others make ornaments for their Christmas tree (*behind pole*).

Indy, Remy, and Barthelemy support Major Boucher as he collapses.

A rented steamboat carries the men down the Ogooué River, toward their destination, Port-Gentil.

The Ubangi boy mops the brow of his injured friend Barthelemy.

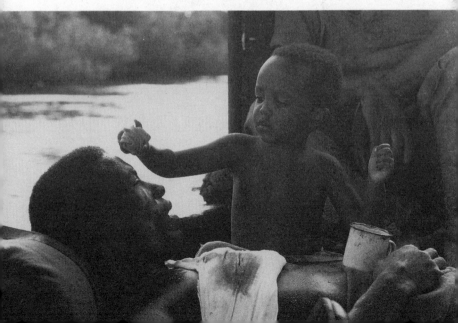

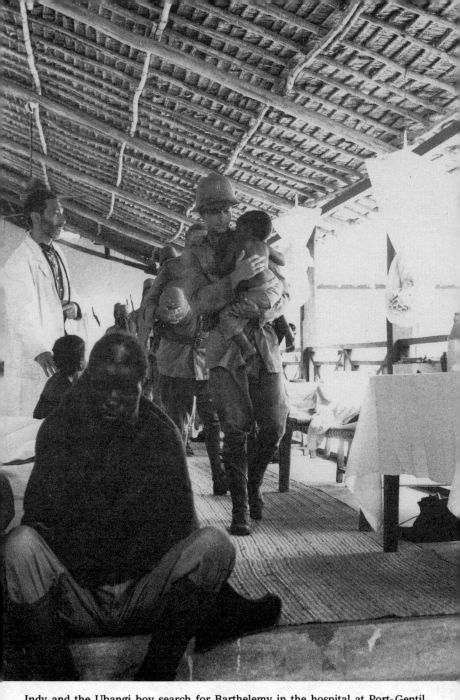

Indy and the Ubangi boy search for Barthelemy in the hospital at Port-Gentil.

Chapter 8

That evening Indy and Remy sat by a camp-fire eating dinner—what there was of it. They had finished a brown substance that was beef stew, according to the label on the can. Now they were on dessert—freshly picked jungle fruit.

Remy looked at the fruit on his tin plate and shook his head. "You know, in France a fancy restaurant would charge a fortune for exotic fruit like this. But right now I'd trade all the fruit in the jungle for a plateful of what you

Americans call French fried potatoes. Let me tell you, the French fries we make in Belgium are even better—the best in the world."

Remy approached eating fruit the European way, with a knife and a fork. He sliced a piece, speared it, then paused with his fork halfway to his mouth. "I wonder if I will ever eat any *pommes frites* again in my favorite Brussels café. I wonder if I will ever see Brussels again." He looked at Indy, who was poring over a map with compass and protractor in hand. "Hey, my friend, how far to go before we reach civilization?"

"That's what I'm trying to figure out," Indy said. "According to Boucher, we're *here*," and he pointed at a mark he had made on the map. "But when I make my own calculations, I put us down here somewhere," and he moved his finger down the map until it went past the edge. There were more than four inches between the two marks. That meant sixty kilometers. More than thirty-six miles.

Remy put down his fork, fruit untasted. "That's a couple of days' march difference. You and Boucher better get together and decide what's what and who's where. The last thing I want to be is lost. Every day in this jungle seems like an eternity."

"I have to make absolutely sure I'm right before I go to Boucher," Indy said. "You know the major."

Remy nodded. "Right. He'll listen to reason. But only if you have it spelled out in letters a mile high."

Indy stared hard at his map. "If I only had some other maps, bigger ones, to check out, then maybe—"

"Sergeant Barthelemy has maps," Remy said. "I saw him looking at them a couple of days ago. You're not the only one who has some doubts about our leader."

"Yeah," said Indy. "Barthelemy definitely has a mind of his own. Though he's careful to keep it under wraps."

"Can't say I blame him," Remy said. "As far as I can see in Africa, any native who sticks out from the crowd risks getting cut down to size fast."

"Getting cut down to size—or getting cut down, period," said Indy. He had heard that the Belgians dealt with native unrest much more harshly than the Germans did. The Belgians took no prisoners. "I think Barthelemy trusts us, though. He might let us see his maps and his markings."

"I'll see if I can borrow them," Remy said. He got to his feet and headed to where the askaris were camped, well away from the officers.

After he left, Indy continued staring at his map. But his mind was not on it. His mind was on Barthelemy. And the other natives. And the Belgians. And this war they were in and the land where it was being fought.

He had come to Africa thinking it was something like America in the days of the pioneers. A big empty place that farmers and ranchers and miners could make something of. Oh, he knew that some bad things had been done to the native American Indians who were already there, that they had been pushed around. But, still, he thought of his country as pretty much up for grabs when the settlers came.

He couldn't think of Africa that way anymore—not after having had a good look at it. There were simply too many natives and too few Belgians. The Belgians didn't seem interested in settling the land, just in running it. The same way you ran a business. To make a profit.

That was one idea of his that had changed. The other idea was about the war here. In Europe, they said this war was about freedom. Indy had thought the same thing was true in Africa. But he was beginning to see that Boucher's ideas were closer to the truth. Belgium was willing to shed blood for the land they had and whatever they could grab from the Germans. But the only freedom in Africa that the Belgians seemed to be fighting for was the freedom to keep on doing just what they wanted.

Indy scratched his head.

Where did that leave him, under Belgian orders, while commanding native troops?

Which side was he on? He honestly didn't know. He'd have to play it by ear.

Suddenly he heard Remy's voice. Just barely. It was low, a shade above a whisper. "Indy? Could I have a word with you?"

Indy looked up. "What is it? Where are the maps?"

Remy kept his voice down. He indicated with his eyes that Arnaud and LaFleur were within earshot in the next tent. He wanted to keep what he had to say private. "I think we have a little problem."

"A little problem?" said Indy.

"A little problem," Remy repeated. "You'd better come take a look at it yourself."

"Okay. If you say so," said Indy, and got to his feet. He followed Remy through the jungle to where the askaris were camped.

Remy opened the flap of a tent and quickly pulled Indy inside.

It was Sergeant Barthelemy's tent. Barthelemy was squatting on the dirt floor. In one hand was a mess tin of mashed fruit. In the other was a battered spoon heaped high with some of it. And sitting next to him was a small child happily gumming a mouthful of fruit.

"Congratulations," said Remy dryly. "It's a boy."

Indy shook his head as if he had taken a left hook out of nowhere. "Oh, my God. He brought the kid from the village." Indy turned to Barthelemy. "Where have you been keeping him?"

"With de bearers, at de rear," Barthelemy replied, not bothering to get up. He met Indy's accusing stare squarely, unafraid. "What you do to me now, Cap'n?"

"Damn it, Sergeant!" said Indy angrily. "I can't believe you'd put me in this position!"

"You not be blamed," Barthelemy said calmly. "You did not know I took de boy."

"But I am responsible," Indy said grimly. "As an officer, I am responsible for anything my men do. I am responsible for knowing everything they do. I am responsible for making sure they obey orders. And when Boucher has you shot— that will also be my responsibility." He turned to Remy. "Keep an eye on them."

It was Remy's turn to look stunned. "Where are you going, Indy?"

But Barthelemy already knew the answer. "You go to de majuh, right, Cap'n Indy? You do your job the same like all white men do. You turn me in. I right or I wrong?"

Indy had to force his words out. "You're right."

Barthelemy didn't wince. His hand stayed steady as a rock as he fed the little boy another spoonful of mashed fruit. The boy took it eagerly.

"But you can't," Remy protested, speaking to Indy but with his eyes on Barthelemy and the child.

"I can. I have to. And I will," Indy said.

Chapter 9

There was a dead silence in Barthelemy's tent—except for the happy gurgling of the little boy as he ate.

Everybody else's eyes were on Indy as he tried to explain.

"We can't hide this," he said. "Boucher is bound to find out about the boy. It's best if I go tell him. I'll figure out a story that might satisfy him. I'll try to smooth things over. Make some kind of deal."

"Make a deal? Wid de majuh?" said Barthelemy, shaking his head.

"Don't worry. If there's anyone who can do it, it's Indy," said Remy, trying to be optimistic. "I've seen him get out of tighter spots than this. He's got a genius for it."

"Sure," Indy said, keeping up the upbeat mood. "I can wind Boucher around my little finger with one hand tied behind my back."

"One thing I like about you, Cap'n," Barthelemy said. "You tell good jokes."

But Barthelemy wasn't laughing. Or even smiling. There wasn't a spark of hope in his eyes as he watched Indy leave.

By the time Indy entered Boucher's tent, he had lost his jaunty stride. It wasn't exactly like charging a machine gun. It was more like walking into the mouth of a cannon.

He found Boucher wrapped in a blanket, shivering. Nearby, Captain LaFleur was brewing him some tea.

Nervously Indy cleared his throat.

Boucher looked up. "I'm not feeling well. Is it important?"

"Yes, sir," Indy said, and hesitated. "Well, kind of."

"*Is* it, or *isn't* it?" Boucher demanded.

Indy had gotten off on the wrong foot. Trouble was, there was no way to go back and start again. He had to plunge straight ahead.

"It's the child, sir, from the village we passed through," Indy said. "He's—" Indy swallowed hard, then went on. "He's here, in camp."

Boucher's spine became ramrod straight. His eyes glowered. His voice rasped with rage. "*Who disobeyed my orders?*"

Indy decided that this was not the best time to come even close to telling the truth. He had to come up with something better—fast.

"Sir," he said, "it seems the boy followed us. The bearers at the rear of the column took him in. Sergeant Barthelemy discovered the child's presence and reported it to me."

"I see," Boucher said—in a way that told Indy that Boucher could see more than Indy wanted him to.

Quickly Indy strengthened his cover story. "The bearers were unaware of the order, sir. I failed to make it known to them. The fault is mine. I accept full responsibility."

"Commendable," Boucher said dryly. "Then you can also accept responsibility for making sure that the child does not move out with us tomorrow morning."

Indy gulped. "Sir, if I may? The boy has come this far. He seems in good health."

Boucher's mouth curved in a particularly nasty smile. "Let us get some expert opinion. Captain LaFleur, how healthy do you think a child from that village could be?"

LaFleur shrugged. "If he were sick, I daresay he'd be showing symptoms by now. Most likely be dead, in fact."

Boucher's eyes blazed. "I do not want a *guess*, Captain. Can you assure me without a shred of doubt—staking all our lives on the answer—that that child is not a carrier of a deadly disease?"

LaFleur retreated in the face of Boucher's fury. His reply was close to a mumble. "I can't say with absolute certainty. Not out here. Not without proper equipment."

Boucher turned triumphantly to Indy. "You have your answer, Captain. The rational decision. Leave the boy behind. Tie him to a tree if you have to."

One look at Boucher's face, and Indy knew there was nothing more to say.

Nothing except, "Yes, sir."

That was hard enough to do. But it was even harder to show his face back in Barthelemy's tent.

"What happened with the major?" Remy demanded anxiously.

Indy tried to break the news gently. "The veins in his forehead started bulging. I thought his head would explode. So I lied."

"Good policy," Remy said. "It usually works."

But Barthelemy wasn't swallowing small talk. "What of the chil'?" he asked.

Indy stiffened. No more beating around the bush. "He can't come with us," he said. He used his most grown-up voice—a voice that made him sound like a stranger even to himself. "I'm sorry. The major was very firm."

"Majuh Boucher very bad! Very evil," said Barthelemy, not even trying to mask the deep anger bubbling up from deep within him.

Indy tried to cool him down. "The major is trying to do what's best for *all* the men, including you."

"Killing boy best for Barthelemy?" demanded the sergeant. "Make me better soldier?"

"That's not what I meant," Indy declared, trying not to sound as feeble as he felt.

"Majuh Boucher only care what best for Majuh Boucher!" Barthelemy pressed on. "Only care best for *his* people."

Indy tried to come up with an answer to that. He ransacked his brain. All he could find were ideas that he had believed in once but that now felt like clothes from childhood, far outgrown.

"He cares about your people, too," Indy said, his words hollow. "That's why he's here. That's why we're all here. To get the Germans out of Africa so your people can have a future."

Barthelemy stared at Indy. Then he laughed. A terrible laugh. "Cap'n Indy. You very good man. Kind man. But not *smart* man."

Indy felt himself shrinking under Barthelemy's gaze. He got smaller and smaller, until he felt as small as one of the cockroaches scurrying on the tent floor.

But Indy had to listen as Barthelemy went on. "Belgian not here for my people future! When dis war over, Belgian go home? No. Belgian want to own African soil, same as German! No difference."

How could Indy argue, when he had been thinking the same things himself? At this moment he almost envied someone like Boucher.

A closed mind made life so nice and simple. Thinking made everything so complicated.

The best he could do was fall back on the idea of duty. "How can you say that?" Indy demanded. "You're a sergeant in the Belgian army. You've sworn to serve the Belgian flag."

Barthelemy nodded, his mouth a bitter line. "Belgian white man come and took me from my village and made of me a white man's soldier. Took *all* young men, all be white man's soldier. My family hungry, I not there to feed them. I am here, fight *your* war. Maybe die. When war over, Africa still not belong to *my* people."

"My God, he's a separatist," Remy gasped.

Barthelemy ignored his shock. "You cannot make future for my people. Belgian, French, German . . . all de same." Barthelemy stooped over, picked up the little boy, and held him high, to the child's delight. "Here is *my* people future. Every chil'. If dey grow strong . . . wise . . . dey make future for my people. Not be white man's soldier in white man's Africa . . . but *black* man, *African* man, in *his* Africa! You savvy me, Cap'n?"

Before Indy could answer, the little boy wriggled down from Barthelemy's grasp. He went straight to Indy and began playing peekaboo with him. A grin lit Indy's face. The child laughed and said a few words of what sounded like baby talk.

"I don't understand much Ubangi," Indy said.

"He say, you be his friend?" Barthelemy translated.

Indy looked at the little boy.

Indy looked at Barthelemy.

"I have my orders," Indy said softly.

Chapter 10

The next day at dawn Major Boucher saw how well Indy had followed his orders.

First a bugle call split the air, drowning out the cawing of wakening birds and the incessant humming of insects.

Then the askaris assembled in a rough column—a column far more ragged than when the trek had started so long ago and so far away.

Finally the major emerged from his tent. He was as spick-and-span as ever. His face, though, was shiny with sweat, and his eyes were strangely bright. He made an effort to focus them as he inspected the troops.

He gave one quick glance, then turned to Indy, who stood beside him with the other officers.

"Where is Sergeant Barthelemy?" Boucher demanded. "He should have been the first man in formation. The fellow's getting slack. Never fails. Give a native a few stripes on his sleeve, and he starts losing discipline."

Indy had an uneasy feeling in the pit of his stomach. He turned to Remy. "Where *is* Barthelemy?"

Remy looked uneasy too. "I haven't seen him."

Then Barthelemy came into sight. He came from around the end of the line of soldiers, and moved toward his position at the head.

"About time, Sergeant," Boucher barked as Barthelemy approached. "Now let's move out!"

Then he froze, his mouth hanging open.

Holding Barthelemy's hand, half-trotting to keep up, was the little boy from the village.

Sputtering, Boucher wheeled to face Indy. "Captain, did we suffer some miscommunication last night?" he spat out.

"No, sir," Indy said weakly.

"Give the men the order: Eyes front, facing

me," Boucher snarled, striding down the column.

"Ten'shun! Left face!" Indy bellowed.

The column of men stiffened as one, and swung around to form a solid wall facing the major. Indy stayed at Boucher's side.

With grim deliberation, Boucher moved along the line of men until he stood directly in front of Barthelemy and the boy.

"This is a dangerous game you're playing with me, Sergeant," Boucher told him.

"Suh, dis boy not sick," Barthelemy replied.

"Thank you for your diagnosis," Boucher said, clearly struggling to keep his rage under control. *"Now hand him over."*

Barthelemy didn't move. "He come wid us," the sergeant calmly said.

Indy, standing beside Boucher, could almost *hear* the major's self-control snap like a brittle twig.

"By God, I will be obeyed!" he screamed.

With that he made a grab at the terrified little boy. He seized the boy's arm. But the boy clung with his other hand to Barthelemy's iron grip.

For a fearful moment, there was a tug-of-war

that seemed intended to tear the little boy in two.

Swiftly and suddenly it ended.

Barthelemy's free hand, huge and powerful, slammed against the major's chest, breaking his hold and sending him staggering back. Soothingly Barthelemy picked up the little boy and cradled him in his arms.

Boucher stood still a moment, shaken to his core. Not so much from the shove. But from the very idea of who had delivered it.

Barthelemy had done what no native should do. What no native could possibly be allowed to do.

He had dared to disobey a Belgian officer. And even more incredible, he had actually used physical force on his superior.

When Boucher found his voice, that voice went beyond simple rage. It sounded close to madness. "My men are perishing in the jungle like dogs!" he screamed. "This is treason, Sergeant! Vile treason."

Boucher's eyes were blazing as he turned to Indy. "Captain, draw your sidearm and take aim at the sergeant! If he refuses me again—*shoot him!*"

Automatically Indy started to obey. His hand went to the flap of his pistol holster. There it stopped.

"But, sir, I—" Indy stammered, searching for a way to bring Boucher back to his senses. "He's my sergeant. We need—"

"That is not your concern," Boucher said, still boiling over. "*I* am your concern. Now draw your weapon."

Indy didn't reply. He didn't have to. His pistol stayed in its holster.

"It seems I'll have you up on charges after all, as I should have done the first time you disobeyed me," Boucher said. Then he commanded Barthelemy, "Sergeant, step forward."

Barthelemy obeyed, the little boy still in his arms.

"One last time," Boucher said. "Hand over that child."

The major and the sergeant locked gazes. Then slowly, deliberately, not looking away, Barthelemy shook his head.

"This is not a request—it is an order from a Belgian officer," Boucher said as he unsnapped his holster. In terrifyingly slow motion he drew his pistol and pointed it at Barthelemy's head.

Suddenly an askari soldier stepped out of the line to stand beside Barthelemy.

"Back in line!" Boucher snapped.

The soldier answered in Swahili.

"Private Zimu says he also refuses to continue without the child," Indy translated.

Boucher swung his pistol to point at Zimu. "I said, *back in line.*"

Zimu did not step back. Instead, one by one, the entire line of soldiers stepped forward to join him and Barthelemy.

Boucher's face was beet red now, as if his head were filling with blood. "You think this is a game?" he roared. "You think you can test me? You think I won't shoot you all? By God, I will! I'll shoot every last man!" He turned to Barthelemy. "Starting with *you!*"

The major raised his gun, thumbed the hammer back, and leveled the barrel to point between Barthelemy's eyes.

Still Barthelemy refused to blink.

Boucher was the one who blinked. Blinked when he felt the touch of cold steel pressing the flesh behind his ear.

It was the barrel of Indy's pistol.

Indy kept his voice soft and soothing. "You're

being irrational, sir. Emotions are clouding your judgment. You're endangering the men and putting our mission at risk."

"This is mutiny, Captain," Boucher said through clenched teeth.

"I disagree," Indy said. "Now drop your weapon."

Boucher kept his gun in his hand, hammer back, the barrel still pointed at Barthelemy.

He kept it that way even when he heard the soft click as Indy thumbed the hammer of *his* gun back.

"This is not a request, sir," Indy said softly.

As if lowering a great weight, Boucher lowered the barrel of his gun. His shoulders slumped. Then his hand went slack, and the gun fell to the ground.

The only strength he seemed to have left was in his voice. "I'll have you before a firing squad. All of you."

"Yes, sir," said Indy. "Now, sir, shall we move out?"

Chapter 11

It was raining. It had been raining for a week. It seemed it was going to rain forever. Sheets of rain falling on the jungle. Streams of rainwater pouring from the leaves above. Rain turning the earth to gooey mud. Flashes of lightning split the charcoal sky to send new floods of rain gushing down.

"Merry Christmas," Captain LaFleur said. His voice was a croak. He was lying wrapped in a mud-caked blanket under a crude lean-to. His fellow officers were with him. Major Boucher had a separate lean-to. He wanted nothing to do with the others outside of official duties.

Nearby the askaris had built their own crude shelters for the night. All the bearers were long gone. They had either died or deserted, carrying the bulk of the equipment and supplies with them.

"Take it easy," Indy told LaFleur. "Try to sleep. It's going to be another hard day tomorrow, slogging through this mess."

But LaFleur kept talking in his hoarse voice, his eyes fiery with fever. "How can I sleep? It's Christmas Eve. I'm much too excited to sleep. I wonder what Father Christmas will bring. I remember when I was a kid, back home—" That was as far as he got. The word *home* broke his control. Tears streamed down his unshaven cheeks.

"I know what Father Christmas will bring," Remy said grimly. "More rain."

Remy and Lieutenant Arnaud were decorating a small shrub under the lean-to with a few ornaments LaFleur had brought along. LaFleur took Christmas very seriously.

"Look, we have a visitor," Indy said. "Hi, little fella."

The child from the village had come over to

their lean-to, attracted by the strange activity. He peered curiously at their version of a Christmas tree.

"Ah, a child. That's what our Christmas celebration needs," LaFleur croaked, half raising himself on one elbow. "Here, boy, put the finishing touch on our evergreen."

From under the blanket LaFleur drew a tiny silver star. He dangled it so that it gleamed in the firelight. The little boy approached, drawn by the glow. LaFleur handed the ornament to him, then pointed to the top of the shrub.

The boy looked puzzled for a moment. Then he laughed happily. He went to the shrub and, standing on tiptoe, hung the star on the highest branch.

"Hey, that's one smart kid," Indy said.

Then his gaze shifted from the star to LaFleur. LaFleur's eyes were fixed on the star. His lips formed a smile of pure joy.

But both his stare and his smile were frozen.

Indy felt LaFleur's pulse.

"Guess he got his Christmas present early," Indy said, keeping his voice and his feelings under tight control. He extended the forefingers of both hands and closed LaFleur's lids over unseeing eyes.

The next day LaFleur's body was laid in a hastily dug trench with half a dozen other bodies. In life, the officers and the askaris might still live apart. In death, all shared the same quarters.

"I wonder who'll dig our graves," muttered Remy as they slogged along through the heavy rain and mud.

"There soon won't be anybody left to do the dirty work," Indy said. "The last ones to go will have to rot on the jungle floor."

"Keep up the pace! No slowing down! No slacking off!" The words came from Major Boucher. He was trying to shout. But his voice could barely be heard. He was trying to stay a step ahead of the column, to egg on his command. But now he stumbled and fell to his knees.

Indy and Remy ran to help him.

He shook off their hands. "I can get up myself," Boucher said. "I don't need the help of traitors."

He half-rose, then collapsed again.

By now the rest of his command had gathered around him. The little boy, bundled in a dead soldier's slicker, yanked at his sleeve, urging him to rise.

Boucher looked at the boy, then rasped out a bitter laugh.

"Tell your friend here I can't go on," Boucher said to Indy. "He has to leave me behind."

"Build a litter," Indy said to Barthelemy. "We'll carry him."

"No! I forbid it! The rules still apply," Boucher feebly protested. His last strength seemed to gather in the fury of his eyes.

"You heard me," Indy said to Barthelemy.

Barthelemy nodded. "Yes, sir," he said to the new commander.

Four days later Boucher was still in a make-shift stretcher, Indy was at the head of the column, and the little boy was happily mounted on Barthelemy's broad shoulders as the troops, all eighteen of them, marched into Franceville.

Marched really was not the right word. *Staggered* was more like it.

"Come on, men, straighten out your ranks," Indy shouted at them. "Let's show these towns-people what we're made of."

"Who are you trying to impress?" Remy asked him. "This isn't a town. It's a dump."

Indy couldn't argue. Franceville was a handful of shabby, sagging buildings on the banks of the Ogooué River. A few ragged men and a bunch of flea-bitten dogs glanced without interest at the bone-weary, skeleton-gaunt soldiers straggling by on the muddy dirt main street. At least the rain had stopped. Sun and fast-moving white clouds were reflected in the puddles everywhere.

"A dump maybe," Indy said. "But it's the most beautiful dump I ever saw."

"I'm with you on that," Remy agreed.

"Now to find a boat to get us out of here fast," Indy said.

"Can't be too fast for me," Remy agreed.

Indy headed for the biggest building in town—a combination warehouse and general store. A man in a dirty white tropical suit came off the porch to greet him. He showed a row of blackened, rotting teeth in a sharklike smile before he said to Indy in a strong Dutch accent, "Welcome to Franceville. What do you want? I warn you, no haggling. This is the only store in town."

"All I want is information," Indy said. "Whom can I speak to about hiring a boat?"

The Dutchman leisurely scratched a nasty red skin rash on one cheek. Then he said, "Sure you don't want to buy anything? Maybe some soap? You boys look like you crawled through hell on your bellies."

Indy stiffened. His hand went to his holster. *"We didn't crawl,"* he said.

The Dutchman coughed, took a step backward. Then he said hastily, "There's a dock up the street. Ask for Sloat."

Sloat turned out to be an Englishman. A fat, unshaven Englishman wearing a grimy captain's cap. His boat didn't look in much better shape. A river steamer built twenty years ago and not cleaned since. Indy looked at it and sighed. At least it was still floating. And hopefully the engines worked.

"Mr. Sloat," he said.

"Zachariah Sloat, at your service," the fat man said. "Trader in fine goods. Monkey pelts and English gin a specialty. And who might you be?"

"Captain Defense of the Belgian army," Indy said.

"Don't get many visitors here," Sloat remarked. "Specially them what come stragglin' out of the interior like ghosts."

"My men and I need passage to Cape Lopez," Indy said sharply.

Sloat turned and spit a long brown stream of tobacco juice into the muddy brown river.

"Five hundred miles downriver," he said. "It'll cost."

Wearily, Indy nodded. He had a bag of gold coins given to him by Boucher in his possession. And money was nothing to what this trek had cost already. Indy's jaw tightened. They'd be getting off cheap if that were all it cost from here on in.

Chapter 12

Indy sat in a ratty deck chair on the river steamer as he wrote a letter.

I can't help dwelling on the terrible cost of this journey so far, and on the terrible task we must face upon our arrival. Again in this war I must ask myself: Is it all worth it? Is war ever worth it? It seems such a criminal waste. I can only pray that the future proves me wrong.

Indy paused, nibbled on the tip of his pen, then went on.

I hope that the French at Port-Gentil can provide Major Boucher with men for the return trip,
which may prove even more difficult than the
trip there. In any event, God help us all.

"Who are you writing to?" asked Lieutenant
Arnaud. He was sitting beside Indy, also writing a letter. But he was having a hard time.
Violent spasms of shivering kept interrupting
his writing, even though the air was heavy with
heat and he was wrapped in a blanket.

"To a guy I met years ago, in Egypt," Indy
said. "An English archeologist. Friends call him
Ned, but he signs his scholarly papers T. E.
Lawrence. He's with the British army now. In-
telligence. Working with the Arab tribes, last I
heard. Funny how things work out. Both of us
so far away from Europe, but both fighting the
same war that started there."

"Yes, funny," said Arnaud. But his smile was
a death's-head grin. A shiver shook him again
as he sealed his letter and laboriously ad-
dressed it. With a trembling hand he held it out
to Indy. "To my wife, back in Belgium. Captain, if I don't . . . get a chance to mail this,
would you see to it?"

Indy swallowed hard. "You'll mail it," he said, as convincingly as he could. "We'll be in Port-Gentil soon enough. I don't know how Captain Sloat gets this floating wreck to run, but he seems to do it."

Meanwhile, Sloat was doing his best to do just that. He was sweating over a boiler that was threatening to give up the ghost.

He had to pause, though, when he saw what Sergeant Barthelemy was doing at the helm of the ship. The sergeant had the little boy on his knee while the child held the tiller, playing captain.

"Push the tiller, push it. That's right, that's good," Barthelemy encouraged the boy.

"Sergeant!" Sloat bellowed. "Keep that brat off my tiller! I said man the helm, not use it for a toy!" He turned to a nearby askari soldier. "Take his place."

Barthelemy translated the order into Swahili. The askari nodded, then replaced Barthelemy and the child at the tiller.

A moment later the askari was draped, lifeless, over it. A bullet had torn through his throat.

Bullets were whining through the air like swarming hornets. A din of rifle fire made the river sound like a shooting gallery.

Every soul aboard the ship dove for cover. Soldiers wiggled on their stomachs toward their rifles. Indy crawled to join Remy, who was lying flat on the deck. Both of them had their pistols out.

Cautiously Indy raised his head to see where the gunfire was coming from.

He saw flashes of rifle fire coming from the undergrowth on the riverbank. Behind the gunfire he saw native faces. At least a dozen, maybe more. Indy tried to get off a shot at them. *Crack!* A bullet splintered the railing near his head. He had to duck back again.

"Who the devil are they?" gasped Remy.

"Separatists. Rebels. Deserters. Take your pick," said Indy. "One thing is sure. They're not our pals."

"Return fire!" Remy shouted to the askaris who had managed to get to their weapons.

The askaris obeyed with a ragged volley. Then a barrage of fresh gunfire from the shore cut down one of them and drove the rest back to cover.

But Indy wasn't looking at that. Instead he was looking at the dead askari draped over the tiller. A fresh bullet had smashed into his corpse.

The body slumped to the right, making the rudder turn with it.

The boat was making a sharp turn. It was heading directly toward their enemies' guns.

Indy looked for the man closest to the tiller.

"Sergeant!" he shouted. "The tiller! We're headed for the shore! If we run aground, they'll cut us to pieces!"

Barthelemy hesitated only a second. Then he stood up from where he was crouching. He raced through buzzing bullets to the tiller. He grabbed the back of the dead askari's shirt and tossed him aside. He grabbed the weathered tiller and turned it. The boat started nosing back on course.

Then Barthelemy screamed. A bullet had splintered the blade of the tiller and buried itself in his stomach. He fell to the deck writhing in pain—right in front of the eyes of the little boy. The child's eyes grew huge with terror.

Indy's eyes swung to the shore. The boat was heading for it once again. The enemy rifle fire was a steady flickering blaze now. The attackers could sense the kill.

"My turn now," Indy said to Remy. Keeping low, he ran for the helm.

He was caught in the gunsights of a native warrior rising from the brush like a phantom to take good aim. The man wore a ragtag mix of African garments and the remnants of an army uniform. His rifle was one of the best the German army issued.

But hitting a target moving as fast as Indy was hard. His shot missed. Just.

Indy felt the breeze of the bullet brush by his cheek. But he didn't have time to even feel relief.

Suddenly his face felt as if it were burning up. He went down howling, a haze of red blotting out his vision.

The bullet had punched a hole in the ship's boiler. A stream of scalding steam blasted out, sweeping across Indy's face like the lash of a whip.

Indy tried to see through the pain. He couldn't. He could only hear the rifle fire coming closer and closer. He could hear some of the askaris chanting tribal songs, preparing themselves for death.

Then he heard something else.

Barthelemy's voice.

He was talking in Ubangi.

"Push the tiller . . . push it . . . that's it . . . play the game . . . push the tiller . . ."

By now Indy could dimly make out what was happening. It was like looking through a slowly thinning mist.

The little boy was standing by the tiller, pushing it. Barthelemy was lying on his back, his head raised with great effort, talking to the boy. The boat was turning, ever so slowly, but still turning, away from the shore. It was moving back into midstream, heading downriver again.

The rifle fire grew fainter and fainter, more and more scattered.

Finally it died out completely.

There was only silence, except for the slow slap of water against the ship's hull.

The ship was out of rifle range.

One by one the askaris got to their feet to see what had saved them.

They gathered in awe around the little boy, who was still cheerfully manning the tiller.

Indy went to join them. His face was as red as a steamed lobster, but his vision had returned to normal.

Boucher arrived, too, with the other officers.

Sloat came as well.

"The little jungle rat saved our skins," Boucher said softly, shaking his head in wonder.

Sloat's action, though, spoke louder than words.

Sloat took off his captain's hat and put it on the little boy's head.

Some people might have said the hat was way too big for such a little kid.

But not anybody aboard the ship.

As far as they all were concerned, the hat fit the boy fine.

Chapter 13

"This boat might make it to Port-Gentil, but the question is: Will we?" Indy said glumly to Remy.

"Wish I knew," said Remy, shaking his head bleakly. "This scow has turned into a hospital ship—but with no doctors, nurses, even medicine."

The two stood side by side on deck as the boat slowly made its way downriver. The scene around them was grim. Sick and wounded men lay everywhere. Groaning, coughing, sometimes crying out in pain, and every now and then sounding a horrifying death rattle.

Even Major Boucher had at last surrendered to the sickness he had been fighting so long. He lay with the others on deck, burning with fever. Indy and Remy were among the few healthy enough to try to relieve the suffering. But there was little they could do.

One other person was doing his best to help as well.

"Hey, look at the little fella," Indy said, managing to smile for the first time in days.

"Yeah, he's doing what he learned to do in the village," said Remy, smiling too. "Guess he's a natural at it."

The little boy was squatting next to Barthelemy. He was dripping water on the sergeant's broad bare chest to cool the fever spreading from his crudely bandaged bullet wound.

Indy saw the boy stop his labors and begin to cry. He went to see what was the matter. He gathered the boy into his arms to try to comfort him. As he did, he asked Barthelemy, "What did you say to him?"

"I say I am his friend," Barthelemy said. "I

say I do not wish to leave him. But if I go away, he must not be afraid. He must grow strong and wise. Make his people proud."

Indy gulped. Then he tried to make his voice stern. "Sergeant, under no circumstances are you given leave to die. That is an order—one I expect you to obey for a change."

Barthelemy smiled weakly, and Indy squeezed his hand.

"You're going to make it," Indy told him.

Before he could say more, he heard a shout from the ship's bow.

It was Private Zimu, pointing at the shore.

Indy went to join Zimu, and followed his gaze.

The boat was passing a compound of low, ramshackle wooden buildings. In front of the buildings was a small dock jutting into the river. On the dock stood a white man with a thick black mustache. He wore baggy white clothes and a safari helmet. He was helping natives unload crates from a canoe. When he saw the boat, he gave a friendly wave.

Indy waved back. He saw that Sloat had come to stand beside him and was waving too.

"What is that place?" Indy asked.

"A hospital, I hear tell," said Sloat. "Run by

some bloody German. But I must say, he seems a right friendly enough bloke. Waves whenever I come by."

Not wasting a moment, Indy went to Major Boucher. He was wrapped in a blanket next to Lieutenant Arnaud, both of them sweating and shivering. Both of their faces, once deeply tanned, were now deathly pale.

"Hear that, sir? A hospital. It's a miracle," Indy said eagerly. He turned to yell at Sloat. "Dock the boat! We can drop off our most serious cases."

Instantly Boucher shouted in a voice stronger than Indy thought possible, "Belay that last order, Mr. Sloat. Remain on your present course. I'll not hand over a single man under my command to the enemy."

"But, sir!" Arnaud protested, feebly trying to raise himself from the deck. "It's a hospital!"

"A *German* hospital, Lieutenant," Boucher replied.

"What difference does it make?" Indy demanded.

"They could torture us for information," Boucher said. "One of us could babble in our delirium. If they find out about those guns, they'll have troops lying in ambush up the length of the entire river, just waiting to take the weapons."

"But if we don't stop, more of the men will die," Indy protested. He looked around for someone to support him.

He saw that Arnaud had used up his strength. The lieutenant was flat on his back again, his whole body shaking.

Indy's eyes turned to Barthelemy, who was watching them and listening.

"Sergeant, you tell him," Indy desperately pleaded.

But Barthelemy said nothing.

"I'm issuing an order," said Boucher. "I will not be defied again!"

"The devil with the Germans, and the devil with you," said Indy, looking at the hospital vanishing behind the stern, seeing the last chance of so many men slipping away. "You heard me, Mr. Sloat! Head for the dock!"

Then he heard Barthelemy's voice, "Cap'n! Majuh Boucher is right. You are being . . ." He paused, and looked to the major for the right word.

Boucher supplied it. "Irrational."

Indy could have kept arguing. He could have said that the German on the shore was a doctor, not a soldier. He could have said that they were in French territory, with no German troops likely to be around. He could have said a lot of things, but he knew it would make no difference.

It wasn't that Boucher was burning with fever. It wasn't that Barthelemy was tormented by pain. Even if both of them had been in the best of shape, they still would have given Indy the same answer.

No Germans could be trusted. All Germans were the enemy.

Both were caught up in the madness of this war. And in this madness any attempt at sanity was . . .

Irrational.

Chapter 14

"They're the only winners in this war," Indy said to Remy.

The two were at the ship's rail, looking at the hideous heads of crocodiles rising from the river, their massive jaws opening.

The crocodiles got what they were waiting for. Four corpses today, tossed into the river. The last to splash into the muddy water was Lieutenant Arnaud.

For days the giant crocodiles had been following the boat. Following and feasting.

"Eat up, you fat scum of hell," Sloat shouted at them. "Plenty more where that came from."

Indy looked at the envelope in his hand. He would mail it to Arnaud's wife when he reached Port-Gentil.

If he reached Port-Gentil.

He no longer thought of this boat as a hospital ship. It was becoming a floating coffin. He wondered when it would be his turn to go. He stared down and met reptilian eyes gazing hungrily up at him.

"You'll have to wait your turn," Indy muttered, turning away.

He went to where the little boy was still tending to Barthelemy.

"Good work, little fella," Indy said. "He's still hanging on. He'll make it. We'll all make it."

Just then he heard a shout. Askaris at the bow were laughing and cheering.

The boat was rounding a bend in the river. Coming slowly into view were the low wooden buildings of a town.

Indy dashed to where Major Boucher lay wrapped in a blanket on deck.

"We've made it, Major!" he said. "It's Port-Gentil."

Boucher looked up with glazed eyes. His reply was a confused mumble. "Boat . . . the boat . . . charges . . . must bring charges . . ."

"Relax, Major," Indy said soothingly. "We made it. As soon as you're well, you can bring all the charges against me you want."

He felt the major's forehead. It was burning.

Boucher's hand was icy, though, as it fastened around Indy's wrist. "No . . . no . . . explosive charges . . . can't let guns . . . fall into German hands. . . . You're in command now. It's up to you to get guns through."

"I won't let you down, sir," Indy comforted him. The major was still fighting the imaginary Germans in French Africa.

"Of course you will," the major rasped. "You're soft. Undisciplined. Not fit to command men."

Boucher tried to laugh. But before he could, his last breath escaped his body.

Indy looked down at the major. Boucher lay staring sightlessly at the sun. He no longer had to worry about the Germans. For the major, the war was over.

For Indy, though, the toughest fight still lay ahead. The fight to save what lives he could.

The moment the ship docked, he headed for the nearest French officer. A lieutenant named Marcel.

"I am in command of this mission," Indy told him. "I request that you transport my sick and wounded to a hospital without delay."

The Frenchman shrugged. "Of course, if you think that will do them any good."

It was hours before Indy could make it to the hospital himself. First he and Remy, as the only surviving Belgian officers, had to report to the French commander and discuss picking up the arms. Then they gathered the remaining askari soldiers to make the trip to visit their sick mates. When they got to the hospital, Indy saw what Lieutenant Marcel had meant.

Hopeless confusion ruled. Patients lay everywhere. On the floors of wards. In the corridors. Even in the waiting rooms. All of them suffering. Most of them unattended by the swamped staff.

Finally Indy found a doctor. The man did not look much better than the patients. His face was a mask of fatigue, with a three-day stubble of beard. His eyes were bloodshot from lack of sleep.

"A cholera epidemic—plus an outbreak of

plague," the doctor explained briefly. "Not to mention casualties from fighting in the bush. Restless natives, you know."

Indy nodded. "I know." Then he asked, "I want to see one of my men. Sergeant Barthelemy. Where can I find him?"

The doctor said, "How do I know? You think I have time to learn names?"

"He may have had a little boy with him," Indy said.

The doctor's face brightened. "I did see a boy. Cute little kid. Down the corridor. First examining room to the right."

Indy and the others followed his directions. In the examining room, a doctor had just finished checking out the child.

"Anything wrong with him?" Remy asked the medic, while giving the little boy's shoulder a reassuring squeeze.

"Nothing a few solid meals wouldn't cure. Now excuse me, we're a little busy today," the man said wearily.

"Let's tell Barthelemy," Indy said. He turned to the little boy and asked in his best Ubangi, "Where is Sergeant Barthelemy?"

Grinning, the boy took Indy by the hand and led him and the others to an overflowing ward.

Picking their way through the sick on the floor, they reached the bed where Barthelemy lay.

The little boy got to his big friend first, running ahead of the others. He started talking eagerly to Barthelemy in Ubangi, shaking him by the arm to get his attention.

But Barthelemy did not pay any attention. Barthelemy did not move.

Indy reached Barthelemy's bed. He looked down with a smile and said, "Sergeant. Wake up. You have a visitor." Then his smile faded. His voice was worried. "Barthelemy?"

Two nurses, missionary nuns, one white, one black, came to the bed.

The white nun slowly pulled the sheet up to cover Barthelemy's face.

"I'm sorry," she said to Indy, who was standing still, pale and shaken.

"Please. You'll have to leave now," the black nun said, taking Indy gently by the elbow.

The little boy was crying now, his small body shaken by sobs. He reached out and tried to yank the sheet away from Barthelemy's face.

Indy put his arms around the child and tried to comfort him. "Shh. He's gone. He's gone," Indy whispered.

He spoke in French, the language that Belgians spoke. The little boy had begun to pick it up. He was a fast learner.

"Was he the boy's father?" the black nun asked.

"He was his friend," Indy answered. "The boy has nobody now."

With a burst of strength, the boy tried to break free. His little hands grabbed at Barthelemy's wrist and shook it.

"My friend! My friend! Don't leave!" he cried in his native tongue.

"He's a Ubangi child," the black nun said.

"Do you speak Ubangi?" Indy said.

She nodded.

"Mine isn't very good," Indy said. "Tell him he must never forget what his friend said." He turned to the boy. "Don't be afraid. Grow strong and wise. Make your people proud." Then he said to the nun, "Will you tell him, please, Sister?"

Softly she made the translation.

Still sobbing, the boy buried his face in Indy's neck.

"Poor little thing," the white nun said. "Does he have a name?"

Indy hesitated. He looked around at Remy and the circle of askari soldiers. He read the answer in their eyes.

"Barthelemy," Indy said. "His name is Barthelemy."

The black nun gathered the sobbing boy in her arms. She murmured soft words in his language as she gently rocked him.

"Perhaps you can leave him with us," the white nun said. "We have an orphanage here, with a school. I promise you, we will care for him well."

Indy looked around again. The men nodded.

By now the little boy had stopped sobbing. He stood straight. He was trying not to be afraid. He was trying to be brave. And he was succeeding.

Indy shook his hand.

"So long, little fella," Indy said.

Then, one by one, all the others shook the little boy's hand.

"Okay, men, form ranks," Indy said, and the men shouldered their weapons.

"Forward—march," he said.

It was one of the hardest commands that Indy had ever given and that the askaris had ever obeyed. In disciplined formation, they marched away from the little boy, not looking back.

"I wonder what will become of him," murmured Remy, at Indy's side. "I guess we'll never know."

"Funny thing, I have a hunch we will," Indy said, falling into the cadence of the march. "In fact, I'd bet we hear about him someday."

Indy was right. Years later all the world heard of him, when he became the first president of the Central African Republic, the man who led his people to freedom and even composed their national anthem and designed their flag.

The name Barthelemy Boganda was in newspapers the whole world over. And in history books forever.

Meanwhile, though, Indy still had to lead his men and the shipment of weapons back across Africa, without Major Boucher to command them, and without Sergeant Barthelemy to hold them together.

But that is another story.

Historical Note

Indy's fears about the future of Africa after World War I proved justified. The European countries with territory in Africa showed no inclination to give up any of it. The colonies of Germany, which lost the war in 1918, were swallowed up by the winners, England and France. Belgium kept a tight hold on all of its mineral-rich land.

It was only after World War II ended in 1945 that one by one the nations of Africa won independence, some through negotiation, some through violence. Today the map of Africa is filled with the names of nations that did not exist at the time of Indy's African adventure. Among the largest of them is Zaire, once the Belgian Congo.

TO FIND OUT MORE . . .

Zaire . . . in Pictures (Visual Geography Series). Published by Lerner Publications Company, 1992. Surveys the land, peoples, and history of Zaire—the former Belgian Congo that Indy trekked across. Photos (some in color), maps, and charts.

Central African Republic . . . in Pictures (Visual Geography Series). Published by Lerner Publications Company, 1989. A brief history of the Central African Republic—formerly part of French Equatorial Africa, which Indy journeyed through—including maps, charts, and photos (some in color). Barthelemy Boganda (the Ubangi boy in our story) grew up to become the first president of the Central African Republic.

The Doctors Who Conquered Yellow Fever (Landmark Books) by Ralph Nading Hill, illustrated by R. M. Powers. Published by Random House, 1957. Tells the amazing story of how U.S. Army and Cuban doctors discovered that mosquitoes infect humans with the tropical disease yellow fever—the same disease that killed many of Indy's troops.

Jambo Means Hello: Swahili Alphabet Book by Muriel Feelings, illustrated by Tom Feelings. Published by Dial Books, 1974. A simple introduction to Swahili, the language spoken by many peoples in the Congo, Zaire, and other parts of Africa, and the language Indy spoke to the askari troops.

Ashanti to Zulu: African Traditions by Margaret W. Musgrove, illustrated by Leo and Diane Dillon. Published by Dial Books, 1976. A picture book that highlights a variety of African peoples and their cultures, from A to Z, and presents information of interest to readers of all ages.

Village of Round & Square Houses written and illustrated by Ann Grifalconi. Published by Little, Brown, 1986. A tale from the Cameroons hills in Central Africa about an actual village called Tol, where all the women live in round houses and all the men live in square houses. Indy would have seen these traditional huts in his travels.

There's a world of adventure awaiting you when you join the official Lucasfilm Fan Club!

Go behind-the-scenes on the new television series *The Young Indiana Jones Chronicles* in each issue of the quarterly Lucasfilm Fan Club Magazine. Exclusive Interviews with the cast and crew, exciting full-color photos and more fill every page! In addition, the latest news on the new *Star Wars* movies is found within the pages of the Lucasfilm Fan Club Magazine as well as interviews with actors, directors, producers, etc. from past Lucasfilm productions, special articles and photos on the special effects projects at Industrial Light & Magic, the latest in computer entertainment from Lucasfilm Games and More! Plus you'll receive, with each issue, our exclusive Lucasfilm Merchandise catalog filled with all the latest hard-to-find collectibles from *Star Wars* to *The Young Indiana Jones Chronicles* including special offers for fan club members only!

If you love the kind of entertainment only Lucasfilm can create, then The Lucasfilm Fan Club is definitely for YOU! But a one-year subscription to the Lucasfilm Fan Club Magazine is not all you receive! Join now and we'll have delivered right to your front door our brand new, exclusive *Young Indiana Jones Chronicles* Membership Kit which includes:

- Full-color poster of 16 year-old Indy, Sean Patrick Flanery!
- Full-color poster of 9 year-old Indy, Corey Carrier!
- *Young Indiana Jones Chronicles* Sticker!
- *Young Indiana Jones Chronicles* Patch!
- Welcome Letter from George Lucas!
- Lucasfilm Fan Club Membership Card

Don't miss this opportunity to be a part of the adventure and excitement that Lucasfilm creates! Join The Lucasfilm Fan Club today!

JOIN FOR ONLY $9.95

YES, SIGN ME UP FOR THE ADVENTURE! I WANT TO JOIN THE LUCASFILM FAN CLUB!

Enclosed is a check or money order for $_____

U.S. DOLLARS ONLY; 1 YEAR MEMBERSHIP— (9.95 US) ($12.00 CANADA) ($21.95 FOREIGN)

Charge to my: ❑ Visa ❑ MasterCard

Account # _____

Signature _____

Name (please print) _____

Address _____

City/State/Zip/Country _____

Send check, money order or MC/VISA order to:
The Lucasfilm Fan Club
P.O. BOX 111000
AURORA, COLORADO 80042 USA

© & TM 1992 Lucasfilm Ltd.